Be Responsible

Dear Parent:

What possesses Charley not to heed his father's warning? For that matter, what possesses him to take over the ice cream machine in the first place?

Like many young children and their guardians, Charley and his dad have different ideas about what it means to be responsible. His dad views Charley's responsibility as that of a child who is a temporary guard—not a grown-up store clerk or manager. But Charley is eager to take on grown-up tasks and to show his friends what he can do.

Charley and other children his age typically spend many hours pretending to be grown-ups. Being "pretend" doctors, teachers, storekeepers, etc., helps them to learn, to think more logically, and eventually to grow into adult roles. It also helps them to suspend feelings of insignificance in exchange for a sense of power and competence. Sometimes children get so caught up in their wonderful make-believe world that the boundary between fantasy and fact becomes blurred. A child pretending to be a carpenter loses sight of the reason why he must use only his make-believe tools and not the real ones in a parent's toolbox. The real ones seem so much better that thoughts of parental prohibitions are likely to vanish.

It's difficult to give up the pleasure of feeling like a responsible grown-up and accept the less glorious role of a responsible child heeding parental warnings. That's why we oversee young children, keeping them and opportunities for danger apart whenever possible. Still, we guide them and make our ideas about being responsible clear so that ultimately, our ideas will become their own.

Adele M. Brodkin, Ph.D.

Visit Clifford at scholastic.com/clifford

ISBN 0-439-41200-5

Copyright © 2001 Scholastic Entertainment Inc. All rights reserved.
Based on the CLIFFORD THE BIG RED DOG book series published by Scholastic Inc. TM & © Norman Bridwell.
SCHOLASTIC, CARTWHEEL BOOKS, and associated logos are trademarks and/or registered trademarks of Scholastic Inc. CLIFFORD, CLIFFORD THE BIG RED DOG, CLIFFORD & COMPANY, and associated logos are trademarks and/or registered trademarks of Norman Bridwell.

Library of Congress Cataloging-in-Publication Data is available

10 9 8 7 6 5 4 3 2   01 02 03 04 05 06

Printed in the U.S.A.   24
First printing, October 2001

Clifford THE BIG RED DOG®

The Wild Ice Cream Machine

Adapted by Kalli Dakos

Illustrated by Carolyn Bracken and Steve Haefele

Based on the Scholastic book series "Clifford The Big Red Dog" by Norman Bridwell

From the television script
"Screaming for Ice Cream"
by Sheryl Scarborough and Kayte Kuche

Cartwheel
·B·O·O·K·S·®

SCHOLASTIC INC.

New York   Toronto   London   Auckland   Sydney   Mexico City
New Delhi   Hong Kong

Clifford cools in the water
On a hot summer day,
While Emily and Charley
Race down the dock to play...

A game of hockey,

Using brooms as sticks,

With a trash-lid puck

Clifford catches double-quick.

Here comes Cleo,

And here comes T.

Nice catch, Clifford!

Good job! Yippee!   *Now send it back.*

Ready? One, two, three!

Clifford shoots the lid
As Charley's dad joins the scene.
"Great shot, Clifford!
You have quite a team."

"But it's time for me to go
To the doctor today."

Then Charley starts to beg:
"Oh, *please* let us stay."

"I guess that would be fine,
But keep an eye on the store.
And if you need some help,
Ask Ms. Kit next door."

A little while later,
Charley walks to the machine.
"Emily, I can work the lever
And get us some ice cream."

"Are you sure it's okay?"
Asks Emily. "We're alone."
"Of course," answers Charley
As he makes her a cone.

A tourist sees the cone:

"I'd like one of those."

But Emily shakes her head:

"Sorry, but we're closed."

Then Charley steps in:

"I think it would be fine

If I made you a cone;

I help Dad all the time."

Emily is worried

As the ice cream flows.

But the man takes the cone

And pays as he goes.

"Whooooa!" yells Charley.

"Look what's heading our way!

A big group of tourists—

We'll need some help today."

Cleo serves the cones
From a tray on her head.
T-Bone takes the money,
And the tourists are fed.

Clifford flaps his ears

Like a giant fan at work.

Everyone is happy—

Till the machine goes berserk.

"Charley, turn it off!"

Cries Emily. "Yuck!"

"I can't!" Charley cries.

"The lever is stuck!"

Emily gets some cones—

Empty ones—in a tray.

But they fill up so fast—

She must give them away.

Nearby stands Cleo,

With ice cream to her knees.

Emily hands her the tray.

"Quick! Get rid of these!"

But the tourists are gone—
And not to be seen!
So Charley opens his mouth
And *eats* the ice cream!

"We can't eat it all!"
Emily says with a frown.
But Cleo wags her tail
And starts to slurp it down!

T-Bone trots in

And slips on his feet.

What's going on, Cleo?

Don't ask, T-Bone! Eat!

Emily shouts, "Charley,
Ask Ms. Kit for help!"
But he yells back, "No!
I can handle it myself."

Clifford slips and slides
Into the snowy scene,
But he can't fix the lever
Or stop the ice cream.

Cleo and T-Bone
Slide to and fro.
They romp and laugh
In the ice cream snow.

Cleo plops down
On the trash can lid.
With help from Clifford,
She happily skids...

Across the snowy dock

On the ice cream slide.

Then T-Bone jumps and shouts,

"It's my turn for a ride!"

Then Emily says,
"We have to fix it now."
But Charley shakes his head:
"I wish I knew how."

"*I* know how to stop it!"
His dad appears with a frown.
"Now watch me lift it up
Before I push it down."

And finally—oh, finally—

With one last drop,

The ice cream machine

Gurgles to a stop.

"Charley, if you needed help,
You should have asked Ms. Kit."

"Sorry, Dad. I really thought
That I could handle it."

"You've learned a lesson—
A good one for today.
Now get to work, and clean
This ice cream mess away."

"I'll never eat a cone again,"

Says Emily with a sigh.

"Me, neither," answers Charley.

"If I look at one, I'll cry."

"Me, neither," add Cleo
And T-Bone from the floor.
"Not me!" says Clifford.
"I hope they spill some more!"

Soon the dock is clean,

Except for one last glop.

But Clifford slurps it up—

Like a big red mop.

BOOKS IN THIS SERIES:

Welcome to Birdwell Island: Everyone on Birdwell Island thinks that Clifford is just too big! But when there's an emergency, Clifford The Big Red Dog teaches everyone to have respect—even for those who are different.

A Puppy to Love: Emily Elizabeth's birthday wish comes true: She gets a puppy to love! And with her love and kindness, Clifford The Small Red Puppy becomes Clifford The Big Red Dog!

The Big Sleep Over: Clifford has to spend his first night without Emily Elizabeth. When he has trouble falling asleep, his Birdwell Island friends work together to make sure that he—and everyone else—gets a good night's sleep.

No Dogs Allowed: No dogs in Birdwell Island Park? That's what Mr. Bleakman says—before he realizes that sharing the park with dogs is much more fun.

An Itchy Day: Clifford has an itchy patch! He's afraid to go to the vet, so he tries to hide his scratching from Emily Elizabeth. But Clifford soon realizes that it's better to be truthful and trust the person he loves most—Emily Elizabeth.

The Doggy Detectives: Oh, no! Emily Elizabeth is accused of stealing Jetta's gold medal—and then her shiny mirror! But her dear Clifford never doubts her innocence and, with his fellow doggy detectives, finds the real thief.

Follow the Leader: While playing follow-the-leader with Clifford and T-Bone, Cleo learns that playing fair is the best way to play!

The Big Red Mess: Clifford tries to stay clean for the Dog of the Year contest, but he ends up becoming a big red mess! However, when Clifford helps the judge reach the shore safely, he finds that he doesn't need to stay clean to be the Dog of the Year.

The Big Surprise: Poor Clifford. It's his birthday, but none of his friends will play with him. Maybe it's because they're all busy. . . planning his surprise party!

The Wild Ice Cream Machine: Charley and Emily Elizabeth decide to work the ice cream machine themselves. Things go smoothly. . . until the lever gets stuck and they find themselves knee-deep in ice cream!

Dogs and Cats: Can dogs and cats be friends? Clifford, T-Bone, and Cleo don't think so. But they have a change of heart after they help two lost kittens find their mother.

The Magic Ball: Emily Elizabeth trusts Clifford to deliver a package to the post office, but he opens it and breaks the gift inside. Clifford tries to hide his blunder, but Emily Elizabeth appreciates honesty and understands that accidents happen.